Elements

Written & illustrated
by
R. Kaur

Published by R. Kaur
Publishing partner: Paragon Publishing, Rothersthorpe
First published 2020
© R. Kaur 2020

Illustrations: R. Kaur

ISBN 978-1-78222-799-1

Book design, layout and production management by Into Print
www.intoprint.net
+44 (0)1604 832149

Acknowledgements

Thank you all for your constant support, guidance and
encouragement xx
(Especially to my precious Bunny Saraa xx)

Index

Dharathi: Earth

Tufan: Storm

Samundar: Ocean

Lata: Flame

Drakhat: Tree

"WE – yes, you and me – are living these adventures together."

Chapter 1

An Enchanted Introduction

You have chosen wisely young reader. Find a seat and make yourself comfortable. May I say once again, you have chosen *very* wisely. Before the eager young reader continues, you must be warned that within these pages lies an entire new world.

Now, perhaps you think you know what I am about to say. I can just hear you now – *"Oh, another story about magical, mystical, alien and heroic tales."* Yes, this is what I would expect from you. As much as I myself enjoy these tales, and even better, am *living* these adventures, this, however, is a story of how *WE* – yes, you and me – are living these adventures *together*. The very adventures which are taking place all around us at this very moment...

I am about to tell you of something that appears dormant, but is in fact an eruption of life. I welcome you all to the undiscovered world of the

ELEMENT CIVILISATIONS.

The *what?* I hear you say. I guess you were expecting a hidden treasure map or an ancient city of gold. What I am speaking of, however, is far more unexpected than you ever could have imagined. All around you, even as you read these very words – from the cleverest scientists, the smartest lawyers, to your teachers and even to your very own knowledge – you have been told that on Earth there exists one civilisation. Humans.

A little complicated this all must sound. All this talk of *Element civilisations*. Adventures all around us? I expect you thought this was a book you could pick up as a little light read.

This, however, is a story for the curious mind; for those of you who enjoy a little more than the odd ingredient of adventure, and magical and comical twists to your tales. If this is you, then I urge you to read on.

I am about to illuminate your minds, as I welcome you to the hidden world of the

ELEMENT CIVILISATIONS.

Chapter 2

Environmental Existence

Away from the hustle and bustle of the city. Away from the honking of noisy engines, blowing out their smoggy gases. Clogging your nose as you take a breath of morning air. Away from enormous factories, billowing up thick plumes of sooty smoke into the dusty air.

Away from all of this, far away on the edge of the countryside, a very different picture is being painted. If you close your eyes and listen, you can hear the rustling of the breeze floating through the trees. It tickles the branches as it passes through. The rustling meets the sweet hum of birds tweeting good morning as they skim the open fields full of crops ready for harvest. The scent of nature wafts around. It is here we find a secret world. In the midst of this tranquillity the four Elements gather...

"Quenchers, Coolers, gather round. *Hurry, hurry.* Tropics hurry up, and finally, Harvesters, are you all here? Good, now I can finally begin. I thought today we could begin with the Moto reading. Is everyone ready?"

Ronita Rooter paused and waited for the usual nod of agreement.

"Then let's begin. One, two, *three.*"

On the count of three there was a simultaneous outburst.

"By the order of the Laws of Nature
Here we all stand
By the great creator
Our environmental maker.
Harvesters, Tropics, Coolers and Quenchers
Working together to keep Earth's natural way.
Hoping one day
For a pollution free day."

There were yelps of glee as the Elements excitedly fist pumped the air. Everyone had a patriotic air to their voices. Soon everyone was hushed and had gathered around again, waiting to be informed of what to do next.

A serious, but welcoming Ronita straightened herself, ready to address an eager crowd.

"Element civilisations, welcome once again. We have gathered from our daily duties to tackle a much larger issue. We work to reduce the damaging effect on the environment caused by humans. Although we know what I am about to say, because of recent events I feel it is important to explain our duties again so we can plan for the problem we are all facing."

The Elements stared at one another. Ronita had never been in such a peculiar mood. Although she spoke in her usual confident tone, there was something unnerving, not just in what she said, but more in the *way* she said it, that evoked a feeling of apprehension throughout the crowd.

Everyone remained silent.

Ronita straightened up to speak.

"Well, as I was saying, the *Laws of Nature* are being threatened more than ever before. This is due to increasing levels of Global Warming, the Greenhouse effect, deterioration of the Ozone layer, plastic pollution and countless other environmental issues.

Your duties are to work unseen by humans to try to fix the damage caused to the environment.

I will begin with the great Element of Wind, the Cooler civilisation."

The Cooler civilisation straightened up. It was very unusual for an Element to point out the job of another, as each worked so closely together.

"Coolers, your job is to sustain healthy levels of air. This is a very challenging task as air pollution is rising. In spite of this, Breezers and Gusters have worked relentlessly to do so."

By *Breezers* and *Gusters*, Ronita was referring to the two groups each Element civilisation was made up of. It was almost like having two families in each civilisation. Each had its own duty but both had one, overall purpose:

to protect the environment.

The Cooler civilisation was exactly that. 'Cool.' Both Gusters and Breezers were the most chilled out and easy going bunch of Elements you could ever wish to meet.

You would never have believed they were in charge of anything as important as sustaining air across the planet! Breezers worked in the cities, and Gusters worked in the countryside.

Ronita continued:

"Quenchers, dear Quenchers. The Element civilisation of Water – both Droplets and Puddles – work tirelessly together to protect against the effects of water pollution, rising sea levels and water wastage."

Droplets and Puddles looked at each other with great concern. The Quencher civilisation was made up of rebellious and mischievous Elements. If there was ever an Element to 'splash a drop out of line' it was sure to be a Droplet or a Puddle! The Droplets worked in lakes and rivers, while the Puddles worked in the seas and oceans.

"Tropics, the Element civilisation of Fire – made up of our hardworking Scorchers and Humids – you, too, work relentlessly to maintain Earth's healthy level of humidity. This has proven to be incredibly difficult with Greenhouse gases and daily chemical damage to our atmosphere. Nevertheless, you remain focused and have done a marvellous job up until this very day."

The Tropics were hot-headed, temperamental and passionately dedicated to their cause. Scorchers worked in the cities and rural areas, whilst Humids worked in rainforests. At this point everyone was looking even more anxious as there was only the Harvester civilisation left.

"Finally, the Harvester civilisation. The civilisation of Earth. Made up of the Rooters and Soilers, whom I am proud to say I am a part of. Both work to maintain the harvest of food and the protection of crops, and the Earth from chemical damage."

The Harvester civilisation was firm but fair. They were serious, authoritative but incredibly kind. The Rooters worked in cites and the Soilers worked in the countryside.

Ronita Rooter looked around at the Elements, took a deep breath and was about to continue when a small anxious-looking Quencher shouted out from the crowd:

"Ronita, please tell us what's wrong!"

"I never meant to worry you," Ronita continued, almost undeterred by the interruption.

"However, I feel it is necessary to point out our duties because from this moment on, you will need to be rooted in knowing your roles more than ever before.

We fight against human environmental damage for the protection of Element and human existence. As much as it pains me to say, the reality of the situation *must* be faced. What I am trying to say is that the time we've most feared ... *has arrived*. The time has come for us to fight for our

ENVIRONMENTAL EXISTENCE!"

"The Elements murmured agitatedly."

Chapter 3

The End is Near

Silence pervaded the room. Everyone wore an expression comprising confusion and fear. No one spoke. The effect of the silence was exacerbated by the fact that Ronita, after her lengthy speech was also wearing the exact same expression. She straightened up to speak again but no words came out. It was a suffocating silence. It felt as though the last point Ronita had made was literally about to come crashing down on them at that very moment. It felt like the only way to stop it was to say something, anything ... anything at all!

"I ... eerm, well I realise this is a little more than what you were expecting."

The Elements murmured agitatedly.

"A *little* more than we were all expecting? Ronita, I have always had every respect for your good judgement and guidance, but there must be some mistake! It cannot have come to this?"

Everyone fell silent again, and all eyes fell on a restless Guster in the crowd. He wore an expression of seriousness and had spoken with a trembling in his voice.

"He's right!" exclaimed one of the Humids. "There's been no talk of *anything*. This doesn't make any sense. Isn't that right Ronita?"

Everyone anxiously awaited Ronita's response.

"Fellow Elements, as much as I would like to be wrong about this, I could not be more right. I am not mistaken and in no way have I misunderstood the situation."

Ronita Rooter straightened up, closed her eyes and took a deep breath. As if trying to hold back the tears, she quickly opened her eyes and began to speak again. Her authoritative tone had found its place once again.

"Element civilisations the time has come to *FIGHT FOR OUR ENVIRONMENTAL EXISTENCE!*"

She raised a branch to hush the crowd before it had a chance to respond. She continued,

"We work for the protection of the environment. To sustain life for humans, as well as for our own civilisations. Most importantly, we work for the future generations of both the humans and Elements.

Our two main policies have been firstly, to do this through working unseen by humans, as this has been the most effective way since we can remember.

Secondly, we the Element civilisations have succeeded in protecting the environment through *working together*, which is the one thing humans have proved unable to do. Unfortunately, we have not been able to do enough to protect the planet. Earth is deteriorating faster than ever before.

Evidence proves this. The polar ice caps, the unseasonable weather around the world – heatwaves, blizzards, snowstorms, drought – and countless other examples of rapid ***environmental damage***."

"The world was about to end and no human or machine could save it."

Chapter 4

The Official Announcement

As Ronita explained the terrible danger that they were all facing, so too were the humans about to learn of what was happening to the planet.

The President of the United States of America stood ready to address a room full of Ministers, World leaders and TV crews from around the world.

"Ladies and gentlemen, I have called this emergency Global announcement for a reason which can no longer be hidden from the world. Leaders from around the world, including myself and many world experts, have been working relentlessly over recent years to control the problem; but I regret to inform you ..."

The President took a long pause, as if to muster every last bit of energy.

"I regret to inform you that as a result of our misuse of fuel and the development of our industries we have neglected the very source of our existence. Our neglect of our environment has led to its deterioration to such an extent that the effects are now

irreversible ...

*"I will not be taking questions as there is simply **NO TIME**. Our chemical factories, oil wells and countless other human 'developments' have given rise to global warming and polluted the planet so that Earth is no longer able to sustain life. The Elements around us are crumbling and there is **nothing we can do to save it**! The world in a matter of weeks is*

ABOUT TO END!"

Silence pervaded the room. Not even the media jumped up to fire the first round of questions. There were not really any questions to be asked. The situation was *irreversible!* Mankind had created its own downfall. The world was about to end and no human or machine could save it.

"... Earth is no longer able to sustain life."

Chapter 5

The Solution

The Elements continued to discuss how they were going to save the planet. The solution to the problem was clear: the only way to save Earth was to reveal the existence of the Element Civilisations. They would have to work together if they were to stand a chance of survival. This, however, was a risky option. The Elements had always kept their existence a secret from humans because they believed that humans would use the Element civilisations to benefit themselves.

Throughout history humans had made discoveries and used them to benefit their own development, regardless of the fact that it would bring harm to the environment. Unfortunately there was no other choice, but to reveal the existence of the Element civilisations to the human world.

A short time had passed since Ronita had broken the news of the world coming to an end. The Elements were still in deep discussion about whether or not they should reveal themselves to the humans.

For the first time the Elements were in disagreement about what to do. Revealing themselves posed the risk of being exploited by the humans or that the humans may not trust them, and may work against them.

Other Elements believed it was a risk they had to take, but could not decide the best way to go about it. *Who* could they trust? *How* would they reveal themselves?

Well, 'there's always one' – that's the saying at least.

Johnny Puddles. Johnny was 'the one'. Johnny was – how can I put it? – a *rebel*. Yes, a rebel. Johnny was part of the Quencher civilisation. The Element of water. A dedicated, committed and determined young Element. Also rebellious and impatient (to say the least). He was always getting into trouble for breaking the rules.

By breaking the rules I don't mean he disagreed with the way the Element Civilisations did things. On the contrary, if there was ever an Element you could rely on for anything, it was Johnny Puddles. He was a young, dedicated Element. He was also eager for change. He had wanted change for a long time.

"Johnny Puddles ... always getting into trouble for breaking the rules."

Puddles had wanted humans to learn of the Element civilisations' existence for a long time. Johnny believed working in secret from the humans was not effective in protecting the planet.

Johnny was tired of arguing with the Elements about what he thought the Elements should do. He was tired of the Elements telling him it was too dangerous. He was tired of waiting for the Elements to decide whether or not they should reveal their existence to the humans. That is why Johnny had done something about it ...

Johnny Puddles had decided that enough was enough! He could no longer bear to watch any more damage to the environment and had decided to sneak away to find humans who would help the Elements save the planet. Little did this hot-headed young Element realise, he really ought to have thought it through. There were many types of humans, and Puddles was about to encounter a tricky bunch!

Chapter 6

The Rebel Gang

It was a warm spring day. The Rebel Gang were on a school trip to the beach.

"Hush, everybody! We are not getting off the bus until I have complete control!" screeched Miss Control at the top of her screechy, controlling voice.

It was a hot, stuffy day and even hotter and stuffier on the school bus. The children ran up and down the bus excitedly, whilst Miss Control frantically ran up and down after them trying to keep control. The bus jolted to a stop as the driver slammed on the breaks, in relief that the children were finally getting off!

"Watch it Geeks! You know the rules.

Acrylic Girls rule this school.

Shiny nails and sleek long hair.

Get in our way, if you DARE!"

That was the Acrylic Girls, otherwise known as Ash and Miya. Yes, you've guessed it, the class *bullies*. They barged their way to the front of the bus, glaring and scowling at everyone as they passed. Much like most bullies the Acrylic girls demanded attention and power. They pushed passed poor Gavin and Gwyneth, the class Geeks.

The Geeks were the Acrylic Girls' easiest target. Gavin and Gwyneth wished they could stand up to the Acrylic Girls! Everyone, however, knew that the only ones brave enough to stand up to the Acrylic Girls were the members of the infamous **Rebel Gang**.

"Shiny nails and sleek long hair,
Get in our way if you DARE!"

(And that included Miss Control!)

"... We are not getting off the bus until I have complete control."

I know what you're thinking; this class sounds more like a bunch of gangsters, than a class of children. (Between us, there's not much difference!)

As I was saying, the Rebel Gang was a group of four children, each very different in many ways, but all very similar in one way. They were the most rebellious, obnoxious, rude and downright carefree children you were ever likely to meet! So much so that they had formed a notorious gang:

The Rebel Gang.

Their motto was, (yes, you've guessed it)

REBEL!

Now, when I say rebel I don't just mean they rebelled against the rules, and against what Miss Control was trying to get them to do. (Most of the children rebelled against Miss Control anyway!) I mean they rebelled against *everything*. If their parents told them it was time to get ready for school, they'd say "*NO!*" If the teachers said bring in your maths homework tomorrow, they'd say "*NO!*" If the head teacher said good morning, they'd say "*NO!*" And if mum said it's a sunny day today, you've guessed it: they'd say "*NO!*"

(Personally, I think they should have called themselves the *No No* Gang!)

So let me introduce you to the Rebel Gang.

Dharathi was a stroppy, moody teenager who liked nothing more than to while away the hours listening to her favourite K-Pop band. Tufan was a laid back, chilled out boy who was proud of the fact that his motto for life was 'go with the flow man!' Then there was Samundar, an outgoing and aggressive girl, who had to have everything her own way. Last but not least was Lata. A small girl in size, but in no way small in any other way. Loud, sassy and always down with the latest trend. (The Acrylic girls were in awe of Lata.)

These ferocious four made up the infamous Rebel Gang.

"Tufan, Samundar, Lata and Dharathi."

Chapter 7

Puddles Breaks The Rules

Fresh air and sunshine, this was not the Rebel Gang's idea of fun. They'd much rather have been at home playing computer games, and lazing around at home, terrorising kids in the local playground and generally causing havoc!

As the children were sent off to explore the beach, the Rebel Gang found themselves a quiet, rocky corner of the beach to hang out by.

Sitting on a rock Dharathi slurped the last few drops of her drink and tossed the can onto the beach.

"HEY WATCH IT! THIS AINT EASY WORK ER YA KNOW!" shouted an angry voice.

The can had landed beside a pair of roguish youths who appeared to be collecting litter strewn along the beach. They did not appear to be particularly happy about it.

"Doesn't look hard from where we are," snorted Samundar rudely.

"What are you picking up rubbish for anyway?" said Lata, with her nose turned up at them. She rolled up her empty crisp packet and threw it at the boys.

"Oi, stop throwing rubbish at us! We're doing community service if you must know. Got arrested last

week for littering, and now we've been told to collect filthy litter off this beach for a month! You lot will be in the same boat if you're not careful."

The youths chuckled to themselves as they walked off into the distance. They were the *Terrible Twins*, Tim and Tom, the local youths, who were always up to no good.

"Oi, stop throwing rubbish at us!"

If they weren't busy tipping dustbins onto people's driveways or vandalising park benches, they'd be terrorising old ladies crossing the road. They were a frightful pair, and a frightful sight to match! Not a brain cell they could share between them to give them an ounce of common sense.

"I'm bored, let's get out of here, before that old boot, Miss Control catches us," said Tufan, as he woke up from another one of his lazy naps. As he yawned his long, lazy yawn, he kicked the gang's empty lunch packets, tubs and cartons off the rocks from where they were sitting.

"OUCH!" said a small voice from behind a rock.

The children spun around to see where the voice had come from. As they turned, they saw the most incredible sight. Dharathi toppled off the rock and landed with a thud on the sand.

"Serves you right!" said the voice.

"What ... are ... y..you?" spluttered Dharathi.

"I'm Puddles! Johnny Puddles is my full name."

The most curious creature stood in front of them.

"What *are* you?" repeated Tufan.

"The question is not who am I, but *who* do you think *you* are? Tossing your litter around like that!"

Puddles was trying to hide his nerves.

"Anyway, I erm, well ... I shouldn't really be speaking to you. If the Elements knew I was here, there would blow an absolute storm! We're not supposed to be seen by humans. It's against the Element rules.

"Who are the Elements?" Lata and Samundar blurted out together.

The curious creature looked around nervously and then said,

"Well ..."

Johnny had snuck away from the Elements, in the hope of getting help from the humans. In his desperation, he had not thought his plan through. (He hadn't really thought of a plan at all.) Johnny had now accidentally spoken to a group of humans, who looked like they had very little interest in the environment. If he did not explain who he was and why he was there, he would risk the Rebel Gang revealing who he was to other humans. There was only one option: he *had* to tell the Rebel Gang who he was and why he was there.

Johnny paused and then, reluctantly, continued.

"Come with me."

Dharathi, Tufan, Samundar and Lata hesitated for a moment and then looked at one another as if to confirm whether they should listen to this curious creature. They nodded in agreement.

Dharathi looked back at Johnny.

"Where are we going?" she asked.

"You are going to the undiscovered world of the *Element Civilisations*."

Before anyone had a chance to utter another word they all found themselves caught in a furious whirlwind. Puddles, Dharathi, Tufan, Samundar and Lata were swept away ...

SPLASH!

With a hurtling thud the Rebel Gang found themselves enclosed in a peculiar bubble. As they got to their feet they looked around and realised they were under water. Beside them stood Johnny.

They glanced at one another and then looked around. It was breathtaking ...

"Where are we? asked Samundar.

"I have bought you to the undiscovered world of the Element Civilisations. Every Element: Earth, Water, Wind and Fire has its own Element family. I am part of the Water Civilisation known as the Quenchers. We are made up of the Puddles who work in the seas and oceans and the Droplets who work in rivers and lakes."

"What do you mean, *work*?" said Dharathi.

"We work to protect against water pollution caused by humans."

"Pollution caused by *humans*?" said Tufan looking bemused.

"Let me show you," said Johnny.

Johnny and the Rebel Gang floated along the seabed.

"This is the damage caused by litter which is thrown onto beaches and into the sea."

Dharathi, Tufan, Samundar and Lata looked up and saw the most heartbreaking sight. As far into the deep expanse of sea as they could see, were clouds of plastic bags, bottles and containers of all shapes and sizes, bobbing around the water. Amongst the sea of litter were sea creatures of all shapes and sizes tangled, fighting to swim free. The litter was actually suffocating the creatures! As the gang looked around in disbelief, they saw a crab fighting to crawl out of a juice can. Its legs were torn. It had cut itself on the rim of the can as it struggled to break free. Beside it they saw fish caught in a plastic shopping bag, gasping for breath. The children's eyes began to fill with tears.

They floated further along the seabed. Johnny pointed into the distance. The children looked up and saw a huddle of sea creatures looking limp and hungry.

"What's wrong with them?" asked Tufan.

"They have no food. The chemicals pumped into the sea have damaged the seabed. The food they rely on to survive is no longer safe to eat."

"That's awful!" exclaimed Dharathi.

"Yes it is," Johnny replied sadly.

"How can we help?" cried the Rebel Gang simultaneously.

With a look of relief, Johnny realised that he had won the trust of the Rebel Gang. The Elements could trust them to help save Earth and gain the help of the rest of the human world.

"Well," said Johnny, "the Element civilisations are unaware that I have spoken to you. They are unsure whether they can trust the humans to work with the Elements to save the planet. I, however, believe that with your help we can convince the Elements to work with the humans. We need humans to realise how much damage they are doing to the environment."

They had decided what had to be done. The moment grew closer to the Rebel Gang and Johnny revealing themselves to the rest of the Element world.

Chapter 8

Coming Together

It was the day of the big reveal. There was no time to put it off any longer. Johnny was going to reveal the Rebel Gang to the Element civilisations. He had asked Ronita to call an emergency meeting.

Although Ronita had asked what the purpose of the meeting was, Johnny had only told her that it was an emergency and had urged Ronita to call the meeting. It had taken some persuasion, but eventually Ronita had agreed.

"Gather round, gather round everyone. Thank you all for coming together at such short notice. Johnny has requested to hold an emergency meeting. He has an announcement to make. Johnny, if you could make your way to the front and let us know what you have called us all here for."

There was silence.

"Johnny ... Johnny Puddles ... where are you?"

Silence pervaded the room. There was no sign of Johnny. Where was he? Expressions of confusion soon turned to worry.

Then suddenly,

"I'm here!"

A small but determined voice called out from the back of the room, as the doors to the hall swung open. The Elements turned to face him. Jaws dropped. Everyone's eyes were wide open with shock. Words could not express the amazement on the Elements' faces. Standing beside Johnny stood Dharathi, Tufan, Samundar and Lata.

HUMANS!

Humans were standing amongst the Element civilisations! A stunned silence echoed throughout the room. Silence bounced from one corner to the next. The ancient rule had been broken. The undiscovered world of the Element civilisations had been revealed.

With every ounce of energy he could muster, Johnny straightened up and stepped forward. As he did so the Elements stepped aside, forming a pathway for him as he made his way towards Ronita. The Rebel Gang followed behind. Beads of water trickled down Johnny's anxious face. He nervously came to a halt in front of Ronita.

Harvester opened her mouth to speak, but before she could utter a sound Johnny interrupted her.

"Ronita, please let me explain."

There were gasps. No one had ever interrupted Ronita.

"I can explain," Johnny continued. "You can punish me for revealing the Elements' existence to humans, but not before you hear what I have to say. There is no time to be wasted and I couldn't bear to wait for you all to decide whether or not the humans should learn of our existence.

I understand I have broken our code, and for that I am truly sorry, but please understand it was to help save us all. *To save our planet.*

"I have been studying the humans for a while now. **These children are our answer.** Elements, you must learn to understand that not all humans mistreat the environment. Some work to protect it, and others are willing to change the way they treat it. It is because we do not see the humans; we only see the negative impact they have on our world. This is why we do not fully understand them. These children are an example of humans who are willing to change their ways to protect the planet. Please let me introduce you all to, Dharathi, Tufan, Samundar and Lata. AKA *The Rebel Gang.*

Ronita stared at Johnny. A stiff, solid stare. Focused and unwavering. An expression that gave nothing away. An expression that plunged through your chest like an icicle. An expression only Ronita was capable of wearing.

The Elements waited in anticipation for Ronita to respond.

Ronita lifted her branch and declared:

"The Rebel Gang, welcome to the Element civilisations."

A weary Ronita broke a welcoming smile and embraced the four nervous-looking children. Ronita turned to address the Elements.

"Element civilisations, although it was not planned, it was inevitable that the time would come to work alongside humans."

Chapter 9

We Are All The Same

Shock, relief and panic darted across the faces of the Elements. Ronita had accepted the humans learning of their existence. Johnny had done it! For Johnny to know he had won the approval of Ronita, meant he had won the approval of all the Elements. They may not have all agreed about what he had done – or the way he had gone about it – but the Elements always came together for the greater good.

*"Our purpose is to **save our planet!**"* Ronita announced. *"By 'our planet' I mean the planet of the Elements and the human civilisations. We have shared the planet for longer than we can remember. Earth has been home to the Element civilisations long before the humans. This is why we understand the importance of protecting it. It is now time to come together. It is time for the human civilisation to learn of the Elements.*

Over the next few hours the Rebel Gang got to know and understand the ways of the Elements. What each civilisation did and how they worked together. The Elements took them to many of the areas around the world that had been damaged by humans. They saw the devastating state of the planet.

Chapter 10

The Meeting

The Elements and the Rebel Gang had finally reached a decision. A Global Summit was to be held following the President's announcement only days ago. There would be world leaders, heads of the Military, Navy, Air force and the *World Environmental Organisation* (W.E.O.) all there together. It was the perfect place for the Elements to reveal themselves.

The doors swung open.

A line of marching officials made their way into the conference room. They seated themselves around a large oval table.

The President of the United States of America stood ready to address them all. He raised his hand:

"Ladies and Gentlemen, welco—"

WHOOOOOOOSHHHHH!

An enormous gust hurtled across the room. A whirlwind thrust its way across the table sweeping everything across the room. The blustery gust finally came to an abrupt stop.

Silence, the wind settled.

There in the centre of the room stood the Rebel Gang and the Elements.

The officials stood around the table, aghast. Absolutely *flabbergasted* was the only way to describe them. There were no words, no sounds, no movement made by anyone.

A few moments passed before the Rebel Gang stepped forward.

"We mean no harm," Dharathi said in a shaky but adamant voice. *"We are here to discuss the problems facing our planet, and ... and these are our friends. May I introduce you all to the Element Civilisations."*

Dharathi held out her arm in the direction of the Elements.

"They are an undiscovered Civilisation who have been around longer than humans. They have come to work alongside us to help save the planet."

A few more moments passed and once the initial shock had settled (well, as much as it could!) the President, Military officials and world leaders exchanged looks. They looked alarmed, but more worryingly, they looked suspicious. The only person who wore a different expression was the General Secretary of the W.E.O. – Professor Drakhat Singh.

Drakhat Singh was a short, plump, sympathetic man, who was dressed immaculately. His appearance was as sharp as his wit, and with an IQ higher than all of the officials put together! Professor Drakhat Singh wore a warm expression, one which put both the Rebel Gang and the Elements at ease immediately. Professor Drakhat Singh held out his tubby hand and cracked open a reassuring smile.

"Professor Drakhat Singh wore a warm expression"

"That was quite an entrance Element civilisations! Well, as Professor of the W.E.O. I warmly welcome you, and am intrigued to learn more of the Elements."

The President of the United States interrupted:

"This is a security breach Professor! These intruders could pose a threat."

"The world is about to end Mr President; I hardly think a bunch of youngsters pose a greater threat to humanity than we are facing right now? It's our duty to learn what we can from these Elements if it may provide us with a chance of survival."

Over the next few hours the Rebel Gang, the Elements and the officials began to learn about each other and the problems they were each facing. Over time it was clear that much like the Rebel Gang and the Elements, the W.E.O. was happy to work with them. Professor Drakhat Singh was ready to support them in whatever way possible.

The problem they faced, however, was the Governments. It was clear the Government leaders were not ready to work together. They did not trust the Elements. Ronita could now understand what the Rebel Gang had explained to her. Some humans worked to protect the environment – but some did not.

Chapter 11

The Rebel Army

Time was ticking, Earth was crumbling. Sea levels were rising; flooding was breaking out around the world. People had been forced out of their homes to look for safety. Unnatural earthquakes, tornadoes, tsunamis were being recorded globally. Transport systems had come to a halt and essential supplies of gas, electricity, water and food were unable to be distributed to cities, towns and villages. Chaos had been unleashed and still the Governments were not willing to work alongside the Elements.

The Elements were in deep discussion about what to do next.

"We have two choices," said Ronita seriously. "Either we continue to try and convince the Governments to tackle these problems together, or we rebel and do what we have to do! Elements believe in cooperating, but for the greater good of both our civilisations we must take action into our own hands! There is no time to waste. With our new friends, the Rebel Gang and the W.E.O., led by our trusted friend Professor Drakhat Singh, *we shall save the planet!*"

Cheers erupted and patriotic expressions met one another. The time had come. They would take matters into their own hands.

Silence fell again and the Elements gathered together for their final motto reading before the rebellion...

**"By the order of the Laws of Nature
Here we all stand
By the great creator
Our environmental maker.
Harvesters, Tropics, Coolers and Quenchers
Working together to keep Earth's natural way.
Hoping one day
For a pollution free day."**

There was very little time to draw up a plan of action. Although the Elements had the support of the Rebel Gang and the much needed assistance of the W.E.O. they still needed more humans to help. Saving the planet wasn't going to be easy. They needed access to factories, oil rigs, water supplies, energy supplies, wind turbine suppliers. They needed to gather a

REBEL ARMY!

Word had got out about the Element civilisations. Who they were and why they were here. As Earth was crumbling, people realised they could no longer rely on their Governments to save them. People were queueing up to sign up to help the Rebel Army. Literally! This included heads of factories and fuel plants right down to the Acrylic Girls and the Terrible Twins! For the first time humans realised the importance of looking after the environment, and they were ready to do whatever it took to save it.

They were ready.

Ronita positioned the Elements. The Elements stood ready in every corner of the world. Rooters in the cities and Soilers in the rural areas. With them stood Dharathi and Professor Drakhat Singh.

The Quenchers readied themselves by the main global water sources. Puddles in the seas and oceans and Droplets in the rivers and lakes. Samundar stood beside them.

Coolers, the Element of Wind. Gusters in the cities and Breezers in the countryside. Beside them stood Tufan.

Lastly the Element of fire. The Tropics. Humids in the rainforests and Scorchers in the forests. Alongside them stood Lata.

Chapter 12

First and Final Fight

Meanwhile Government officials had set yet another summit to discuss what action to take next, but also to secretly discuss what to do about the Elements. The Governments felt threatened by the Element civilisations. Instead of learning about them, and trying to understand the possibility that working together could benefit both civilisations, they decided instead to destroy them.

The Elements and Professor Drakhat Singh were unaware of what the Governments were planning. They had decided to take matters into their own hands. Thanks to the passion and dedication to the environment of Professor Drakhat Singh and the W.E.O., the Elements, the Rebel Gang and the Rebel Army stood a chance of saving Earth.

Dawn had broken and Ronita gave the order to begin the fight to save the planet. With the most unimaginable power, the Element civilisations unleashed their forces of nature. Droplets and Puddles quelled the tsunamis and tidal waves. Humids and Scorchers set their blazing powers to extinguish the rainforest fires, whilst Soilers and Rooters tackled earthquakes that were off the Richter scale. Breezers and Gusters fought to calm the hurricanes and torrential storms.

Their energy was running low, but with the help of the

Rebel Gang, Professor Drakhat Singh and the Rebel Army they relentlessly continued to fight.

Meanwhile, back at the Global Summit Headquarters, Governments had planned to destroy the Element civilisations. They felt threatened by the Elements. They had arranged tanks, troops, naval ships and aircrafts to destroy the Elements.

The Governments had heard that the Elements were fighting alongside the Rebel Gang, the W.E.O. and the Rebel Army, but had not seen exactly what they were doing. They were convinced they were taking over the planet.

The President was to order the strike against the Elements. Tanks, troops, naval ships and aircrafts were positioned ready for attack. The President readied himself to order the attack. The army moved in closer to their positions.

"ATTACK!"

The order was given.

The President and the Governments watched as the troops moved in to destroy the Elements.

As the Government officials watched the military moving in to attack the Elements, they suddenly realised what the Elements were doing. They were shocked. They looked at one another and nodded in agreement.

"STOP THE ATTACK!" shouted the President. "Operation Obliterate the Element civilisations, has been *officially terminated.*"

The Government officials had finally realised the Elements were there to help humans to save the planet.

"I order you to fight alongside the Elements to save our planet!" commanded the President.

The tanks, troops, naval ships and aircrafts withdrew their attack and swooped in alongside the Elements and began to work together with them.

The Governments had finally realised they needed to ***work together***. With the energy and resources of both the Elements and the humans, over the coming months, they could finally see positive changes around the world. Environmental disasters were decreasing and there were signs of natural climate change around the world.

Things were finally changing for the better. The Elements and humans were finally working together.

The question was, for how long? ...

The End

Author Message

As much as I love the structure and routine of day to day life, I also crave for an element of change in each day that passes. I want it to be different from yesterday. For each day to offer me something new. Whether that is in the form of the people that I encounter, in the routine of each passing hour or even experiencing a slightly different interaction with those I see on a daily basis.

Just as I have a passion for life to be ever changing, so too is my desire to evolve my own self.

I feel life cannot offer new experiences if we as individuals are not open to change ourselves.

"NO COLOUR HAS A SINGLE SHADE"

The world is a rainbow of people. Each has their own unique shade.
In my writing I hope to convey the message that we should all embrace what makes us unique, in order for us to blossom as individuals.

In particular, my message is to the younger generation. More than ever this message seems particularly relevant. So many young people struggle to accept what makes them different and do not feel confident enough to express their uniqueness because they fear that society will reject them.
I hope, even in the slightest way, to help people realise their identity is beautiful and they should be proud of it.

It's not just about acceptance - we must nurture what makes us all different.
Only then can new shades begin to flourish.

www.ingramcontent.com/pod-product-compliance
Lightning Source LLC
Chambersburg PA
CBHW051558120626
46551CB00013B/1579